Sponsored Education Program

Misty

Best Friends Series
Book 5

David M. Sargent, Jr. and his friends all live in a small town in northwest Arkansas. While he lies in the hammock, the dogs (left to right: Spike, Emma, Daphne and Mary) play ball, dig holes or bark at kitty cats. When not playing in the yard, they travel around the United States, meeting children and writing stories.

Misty

Best Friends Series
Book 5

David M. Sargent, Jr.

Illustrated by Debbie Farmer

Ozark Publishing, Inc.
P.O. Box 228
Prairie Grove, AR 72753

Cataloging-in-Publication Data

Sargent, David M., 1966–
    Misty / by David M. Sargent, Jr. ;
illustrated by Debbie Farmer.—Prairie Grove, AR :
Ozark Publishing, c2007.
    p. cm. (Best friends series ; 5)

    "Manners"—Cover.
    SUMMARY: When Jo's daddy come
home with a fluffy puppy, bad things start
happening. Misty wrecks the house! The puppy
must learn good manners and good behavior.
    ISBN 1-59381-066-0 (hc)
            1-59381-067-9 (pbk)

    1. Dogs—Juvenile fiction.
[1. Dogs—Fiction. 2. Dachshunds—Fiction.]
I. Farmer, Debbie, 1958– ill. II. Title.
III. Series.

    PZ8.3.S2355Mi 2007
    [E]—dc21   2003099201

iv

Inspired by

my three Dachshunds. First comes Mary. Then comes Vera. And last, but not least, is Emma.

Dedicated to

all children who love Dachshunds as much as I love mine.

Foreword

When Jo's daddy comes home with a fluffy puppy, bad things start happening. Misty wrecks the house! The puppy must learn good manners and good behavior.

Contents

If you would like to have the author of the Best Friends Series visit your school free of charge, please call 1-800-321-5671.

One

A Fluffy Puppy for Jo

Eight-year-old Jo ran into the house with a little puppy in her arms.

"Mommy! Look what Daddy gave me!" she squealed. "He said that she is clumsy and needs to be trained."

Jo set the puppy on the floor. The little dog slipped and fell down. But seconds later, it jumped up and ran into the living room.

"Catch him," Jo's mama said.

Jo giggled. "It's a her, Mama. She's a little clumsy but she's smart. She's a Red Dachshund with long hair." I named her Misty.

Jo ran to find Misty. The pup was in Jo's bedroom, holding Jo's favorite doll in her mouth.

"No, Misty! No!" Jo scolded. "You cannot play with Suzie. She is my best doll."

Jo grabbed one of the doll's arms, but Misty held the doll firmly in her teeth.

"Turn loose," Jo demanded.

Suddenly Misty's feet slid out from under her. As her chin hit the floor, the arm ripped from the body of the doll.

"Oh no!" Jo cried. "Look what you did! You tore my doll's arm off."

The puppy dropped the toy. She ran out of the bedroom.

Two

A Clumsy, Wild Mutt

Jo picked up the torn doll and hugged it. Then she laid the doll's body and torn arm on her bed.

Suddenly Jo heard her mama scream, "Misty! You clumsy puppy! Look what you did to my shoes!"

Jo ran into her parents' room. Jo's mama was holding shoes with teeth marks on the toes. Both pillows were off the bed and lying on the floor. A dress had been knocked off its hanger and was in a heap beside a leather belt covered with teeth marks.

"You better find that clumsy, wild mutt before I do, Jo!"

"Yes, Ma'am," the girl said as she ran from the room.

Jo followed the puppy's trail through the living room. There were overturned plants, broken vases, and scattered books and magazines.

"Oh dear," the girl groaned.

Three

A Well-behaved Puppy

Little Miss Misty was sprawled on the living room floor. She wagged her tail as Jo cleaned up the mess in the living room.

"I love you," Jo said as she held the puppy in her arms. "But we have to set some rules around here. Slow down, and maybe you won't be so clumsy. And don't touch things that you shouldn't. You'll learn."

Misty snuggled closer to Jo and went to sleep.

For months, Jo worked to keep Misty out of trouble. She taught the puppy the meaning of "NO". She cleaned up her mistakes for her. Sometimes she even took the blame for boo-boos.

One day Jo's mama came to get her from school. She looked worried.

"I forgot to put Misty in the backyard before I left this morning. I'm afraid to go home, Jo. That fluffy puppy may have destroyed every room in our house."

Misty met Jo at the door. The girl checked the living room and each bedroom. Everything in the house was perfect. Misty was sitting in the kitchen beside Jo's parents, when Jo returned from the inspection.

"Misty," Jo said quietly, "I'm so proud of you. You are my neat and well-behaved best friend!"